Be Brave, Anna!

written by
JoDee
McConnaughhay
illustrated by
Jill Dubin

For Anna, who loves Jesus. Always trust Him! Love, Mom

The Standard Publishing Company, Cincinnati, Ohio. A division of Standex International Corporation.
Text © 1999 by JoDee McConnaughhay. Art © 1999 The Standard Publishing Company.
Printed in the United States of America. All rights reserved.

06 05 04 03 02 01 00 99   5 4 3 2 1

Library of Congress Catalog Card Number 98-061310
ISBN 0-7847-0895-9
Scripture taken from the *Holy Bible, New International Version*® NIV®
© 1973, 1978, 1984 by International Bible Society. Used by permission of Zondervan Publishing House.
All rights reserved.

STANDARD
PUBLISHING
Cincinnati, Ohio

The room was quiet. The window was dark. The night-light made shadows dance on the wall. Anna was tucked snugly in her bed, a soft pillow under her head. She was very, very, sleepy. So *why* were Anna's eyes wide open?

"Daddy!" Anna cried and ducked under her soft quilt.

"What's wrong?" Daddy asked, coming quickly into the room.

"I'm afraid," Anna said, peeping out at her father's face.

Sitting on the bed, Daddy held Anna's hand and said, "Do you know what I say when I'm afraid?"

Daddy never seems afraid, Anna thought. So she sat up and asked, "What *do* you say when you're afraid?"

"When I'm afraid, I always say, 'The Lord is my helper, I will not be afraid,' " Daddy said. "Now, say it with me and you'll see."

" 'The Lord is my helper, I will not be afraid,' " said Daddy and Anna together.

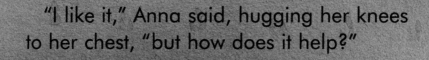

"I like it," Anna said, hugging her knees
to her chest, "but how does it help?"

"It reminds us that God is always with us,"
Daddy said. "And with such a big, strong
helper, we don't need to stay afraid."

Daddy makes me feel safe, Anna thought.
And God is even bigger than Daddy!

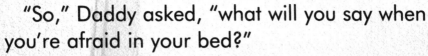

"So," Daddy asked, "what will you say when you're afraid in your bed?"

" 'The Lord is my helper, I will not be afraid,' " Anna said.

"And when you see the doctor because you are sick?"

"I'll say it quick—'The Lord is my helper, I will not be afraid,' " Anna said.

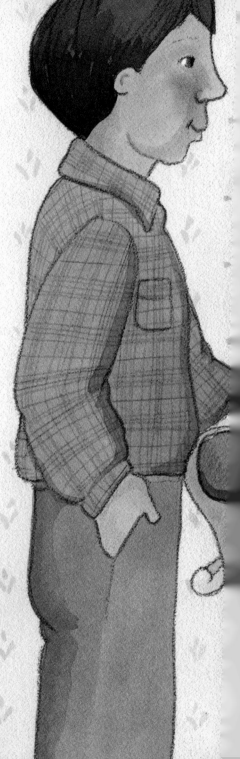

"And when Bethany's big
dog runs over to play?"
"Then I will say—'The Lord
is my helper, I will not
be afraid,' " Anna said.

"And when Nathaniel's cat swats your foot as you walk by, will you cry?"
"No, I'll reply—'The Lord is my helper, I will not be afraid,' " Anna said.

"But what if the thunder is crashing,
the lightening is flashing, and the rain is
splashing outside your window here?
What will you say *then*, my dear?"

Anna snuggled in her bed and said,
"Daddy, I will say loud and clear—'The
Lord is my helper, I will not be afraid!' "
    Daddy smiled, kissed Anna's cheek, and
stepped softly from the room.

The room was quiet. The window was dark. The night-light made shadows dance on the wall. Tucked snug- ly in her bed, a soft pillow under her head, Anna knew—God was there, too.

So she smiled, closed her sleepy eyes,
and said, " 'The Lord is my helper,
I will not . . . be . . . afraid . . .' "

Suggestion to Parents

As your child becomes familiar with the story, encourage him or her to repeat the Scripture phrase with you each time it appears. Then, try letting your child *finish* the Scripture phrase each time it appears. Before long, your child will have memorized the verse!

"The Lord is my helper; I will not be afraid."
–Hebrews 13:6